Cool Dog, School Dog

Have fun with Tinka!
Deborah Heiligman
May, 2009

Marshall Cavendish Children

Marshall Cavendish Corporation, 99 White Plains Road, Tarrytown, NY 10591
www.marshallcavendish.us/Kids

Library of Congress Cataloging-in-Publication Data
Heiligman, Deborah.
Cool dog, school dog / by Deborah Heiligman ; illustrated by Tim Bowers.
p. cm.
Summary: When Tinka the dog follows her owner to school and creates havoc, the children discover a way to let her stay in the classroom and help.
ISBN 978-0-7614-5561-5
[1. Stories in rhyme. 2. Dogs—Fiction. 3. Schools—Fiction.] I. Bowers, Tim, ill. II. Title.
PZ8.3.H4132Co 2009
[E]—dc22
2008029398

The illustrations are rendered in acrylic paint on three-ply bristol board.
Editor: Margery Cuyler
Book design by Anahid Hamparian

Printed in China
First edition
1 3 5 6 4 2

For Julia, Natalie, Amy, and Rick Sams, who were there at the beginning —D.H.

To my good friend, Joe Hickman —T.B.

Tinka is a fun dog,
a sun dog,
a run-and-run-and-run dog.

A joy dog,
a boy's dog,
a chews-a-brand-new-toy dog.

A sigh dog,
a cry dog,
a has-to-say-good-bye dog.

Tinka is a groan dog,
a moan dog,
a hates-to-be-alone dog.

A peek dog,

a sneak dog,

a spring-and-sprint-and-streak dog.

Tinka is a cool dog,
a school dog,

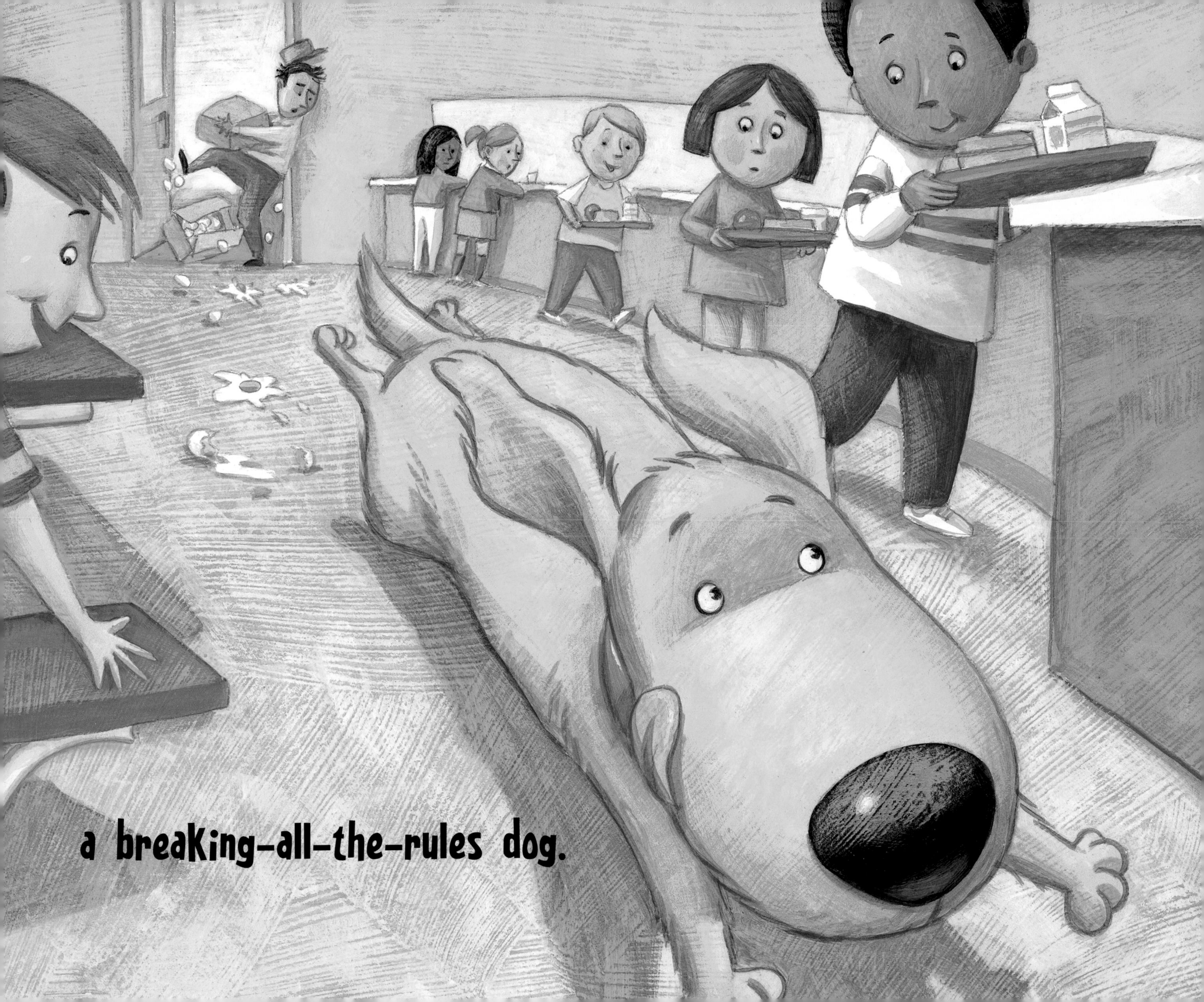
a breaking-all-the-rules dog.

A hall dog,
a ball dog,

a crash-into-the-wall dog.

A vroom dog,
a boom dog,
a messing-up-the-room dog.

Tinka is a bad dog,
a sad dog,
a makes-our-teacher-mad dog!

A “hey!” dog,
a “stay” dog,
a has-to-go-away dog.

OFFICE

A plead dog,
a need dog,
a come-help-us-to-read dog.

Tinka is a sweet dog,
a treat dog,
a-sitting-in-her-seat dog.

READ

A look dog,
a nook dog,
a loves-to-hear-a-book dog.

A yay dog,
hooray dog,

a please-come-every-day dog!